"MARCO . . .

I don't know how long I lay there.

I saw dancing lines of glasses of water. I saw Sam and Fred splashing in a pool.

I cupped my hands to my mouth and yelled some more:

"MARCO . . . POLO! MARCO . . . POLO! MARCO . . . POLO!"

This was it, I decided. The end of the Time Warp Trio. And how weird and wrong that there was only one of the trio.

"Sam . . . Fred . . . Marco . . . Polo . . ." I croaked.

Everything went suddenly dark.
I smelled something horrible. Death?
I kept my eyes closed.
I didn't want to cheat.
I croaked, "Marco . . ."
Someone answered, "Polo."

THE TIME WARP TRIO®

THE *TIME WARP* TRIO® No.16

MARCO? POLO!

JON SCIESZKA
illustrated by Adam McCauley

PUFFIN BOOKS

To Dad and Mom
J.S.

For Kublai "Smitty" Caine
A.M.

PUFFIN BOOKS
Published by the Penguin Group
Penguin Young Readers Group, 345 Hudson Street, New York, New York 10014, U.S.A.
Penguin Group (Canada), 90 Eglinton Avenue East, Suite 700, Toronto, Ontario, Canada M4P 2Y3
(a division of Pearson Penguin Canada Inc.)
Penguin Books Ltd, 80 Strand, London WC2R 0RL, England
Penguin Ireland, 25 St Stephen's Green, Dublin 2, Ireland (a division of Penguin Books Ltd)
Penguin Group (Australia), 250 Camberwell Road, Camberwell, Victoria 3124, Australia
(a division of Pearson Australia Group Pty Ltd)
Penguin Books India Pvt Ltd, 11 Community Centre, Panchsheel Park, New Delhi - 110 017, India
Penguin Group (NZ), 67 Apollo Drive, Rosedale 0632, New Zealand
(a division of Pearson New Zealand Ltd.)
Penguin Books (South Africa) (Pty) Ltd, 24 Sturdee Avenue,
Rosebank, Johannesburg 2196, South Africa

Registered Offices: Penguin Books Ltd, 80 Strand, London WC2R 0RL, England

First published in the United States of America by Viking,
a division of Penguin Young Readers Group, 2006
Published by Puffin Books, a division of Penguin Young Readers Group, 2008

1 3 5 7 9 10 8 6 4 2

Text copyright © Jon Scieszka, 2006
Illustrations copyright © Penguin Group (USA) Inc., 2006
Illustrations by Adam McCauley
All rights reserved

CIP DATA IS AVAILABLE.

ISBN 978-0-670-06104-4 (hardcover)

Puffin Books ISBN 978-0-14-241177-3

Printed in the United States of America
Set in Sabon

MARCO? POLO!

I squeezed my eyes shut.

Darkness.

I called out, "Marco?"

Nobody answered. That was the first bad sign.

I moved off to my right. I wasn't in water anymore.
That was the second bad sign. My bare feet felt sand.

I called out louder, *"Marco?"*

Still no answer. Just something that sounded like
wind. I kept my eyes closed.

"Okay, you guys. I'm not cheating, but I somehow
got out of the pool. And you guys are cheating if you
don't answer."

I twirled around in a fast circle with both hands
out. I didn't catch anyone. And I still wasn't back in
the water.

"Marco?" I called.

No answer.

"Okay, that's it, Sam and Fred," I said. "One more time, and if you don't answer, you are both it."

I yelled as loud as I could, "MARCO!"

Nothing.

I waved my arms in the air all around me.

Nothing.

"I'm opening my eyes."

A warm wind blew around my bare legs.

"I mean it."

I felt sand cover my toes.

"I'm not kidding."

I opened my eyes.

I was expecting to see Sam and Fred hiding in the corner of the YMCA pool in Brooklyn, laughing at me. What I saw couldn't have been more different.

I blinked my eyes. I rubbed them. I looked again to make sure.

I wasn't anywhere near a YMCA pool. I was standing, in my red swimsuit, in the middle of sand. All around me there was nothing but sand. No Sam. No Fred. No YMCA pool. No Brooklyn. Just sand, sand, sand, and oh yeah—more sand.

I was so freaked out, I sat down. (In the sand, of course.)

One minute I was playing Marco Polo. The next I

was standing in the middle of what had to be a desert.

I wasn't sure what had happened. But I suspected it might have something to do with a certain thin blue *Book* covered with silver writing and designs.

I got up and walked around in a crazy little circle. I checked in all directions—sand, sand, sand, and sand. Yep. Nothing but sand. And me in nothing but my red swimsuit. Yep. Not even my flip-flops.

I thought I would go crazy. But I didn't. I had a plan. I cupped my hands to my mouth and started yelling, "Marco! Marco! Marco!"

Nobody answered.

So then I went crazy.

What an embarrassing way to die. Sitting in the middle of a desert in a red swimsuit.

I imagined what people would say:

"Did you hear about that kid, Joe?"

"The one who croaked in the desert in a swimsuit?"

"Yeah. What a doofus."

"What a nincompoop."

"What a—"

All right. That's enough from my insulting imagination.

But before I meet such a stupid end, I should explain what happened before I got here. That will help explain how I got here.

It was getting near the end of summer vacation. August. Not much going on in Brooklyn. Sam and Fred and I had played baseball, basketball, Frisbee, tag, hangout, eat-a-slice-of-pizza-in-the-fewest-possible-bites (three), and all of our video games a million times.

We were sitting on my stoop with nothing to do.

"Wow," said Sam. "Now I know we are getting desperate. Fred is actually reading."

Fred looked up from his newspaper. "Excuse me? It is my job to keep up on some very important box scores. Besides—reading can be very powerful. Here, let me show you." Fred folded his paper carefully . . . and then started whacking Sam with it.

I rolled up the rest of the paper and started whacking Fred and Sam.

Five minutes later, we were back to sitting on my stoop with nothing to do.

Except now we were surrounded by bits and pieces of newspaper.

"Well, that was very mature," said Sam, straightening his glasses.

Fred picked up half a page of comics. "Okay. I will maturely read the comics then. Here's a kid with a dotted line following him all over the neighborhood. His mom says, 'Where have you been?' He says, 'Nowhere.'"

"Who writes those things?" I said. "And do they really think they are funny?"

I picked another half page. "Here's some more lame stuff—horoscopes. These things are never true. Here's mine: Virgo. You will explore exotic lands. Don't forget your hat, your sunscreen, and your horoscope."

"How stupid is that?" said Fred.

"Astrology has been around for thousands of years," said Sam. "It's interesting to think that lives might be affected by the movements of the stars and planets. Read mine. Libra."

I read, "There is something to be said for the loyal and true nature of the dog."

"Okay, that is stupid," said Sam.

"Fred?"

"What?"

"What is your sign?"

"How should I know?"

"When is your birthday?"

"March twenty-seventh."

I read, "Aries. The pen is mightier than the sword. But sometimes the rock is mightier than the pen."

"Amazing," said Fred. "Just about as amazing as the kid walking around his backyard."

We went back to sitting on my stoop with nothing to do.

Sam looked down and read the paper between his feet. "Hey, check this out. The YMCA swimming pool is open today. Free for everybody."

That's how Sam and Fred and I ended up in the YMCA pool in Brooklyn. And that's when things started to go wrong.

We had almost the whole deep end to ourselves. All of the little kids were in the shallow end. The lifeguard wouldn't let us run or jump or dive. So we started playing Marco Polo. That's when things got worse.

Sam hung onto the edge of the pool in one corner. He was wearing the most ugly yellow swimsuit you have ever seen.

Fred hung on to the ladder in the other corner. As always, he was wearing one of his million baseball hats.

And oh yeah—*The Book* was inside a plastic bag in my backpack next to our towels.

Did I tell you about *The Book*? I should. Because when things go wrong—things like finding-yourself-suddenly-standing-in-the-middle-of-a-desert wrong—it's usually because of *The Book*.

This particular book is one dangerously powerful *Book*. I got it for my birthday from my uncle Joe, who is a magician. And the dangerous thing about it is that it can somehow send you back and forth in time, and you have no idea how it works. Well, Fred and Sam and I have no idea how it works. We've never actually read through the whole thing.

We've been warped back to the Stone Age, into samurai wars, and one hundred years into the future. I usually keep *The Book* hidden in my room. But I brought it to the pool to keep my little sister Anna from snooping around and finding it.

Not a good idea.

"Very interesting that the name of a famous explorer would become a game played in swimming pools," said Sam.

"Say what?" said Fred.

"Marco Polo," said Sam. "He was a famous explorer. He traveled from Italy all the way to China and back again. Fifteen thousand miles in a trip that lasted over twenty-four years."

"Very interesting," said Fred. "Joe, you're it. Close your eyes and start exploring for us. And if you cheat and open your eyes, we get to give you five free punches . . . each."

"And if you guys cheat and get out of the pool, I get to give you ten free punches . . . each," I said.

That's when I closed my eyes.

That's when I started calling, "Marco?"

That's when Fred and Sam started calling, "Polo."

That's when everything changed.

I kept my eyes closed, so I'm not sure exactly what happened. But it doesn't take a genius to figure out that the combination of *The Book* and us calling "Marco Polo" time-warped me back somewhere between Italy and China.

But if that was true—then where was Marco Polo?

And where were Sam and Fred?

And most importantly—where was *The Book*?

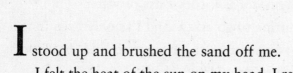

I stood up and brushed the sand off me.

I felt the heat of the sun on my head. I remembered my horoscope.

"Don't forget your hat, and your sunscreen . . . that's too weird," I said. "Oh, man. And now I'm talking to myself. I'm cracking up."

This was bad. Very bad.

I mean, I know *The Book* has warped me into some bad spots before. Like that time we almost got wiped out by Vikings. And that time we had to win a Mayan ringball game or die. And that time we wrestled gladiators in ancient Rome.

But in all of those times, no matter how bad it was, Fred and Sam and I time warped together.

I looked at the red-gold sand dunes in front of me, behind me, to the left of me, to the right of me. I was alone. Completely alone. No Sam to come up with a smart bit of history. No Fred to charge into action. I didn't even have my own usual magic trick.

"I've got nothing but a red swimsuit," I said out loud. "And I have got to stop talking to myself."

The sun beat down on my hatless, un-sunscreened head. I imagined a tall, cool glass of water.

"I'm starting to go crazy. And I've only been in the desert for two minutes. I have got to find *The Book* and get back to Brooklyn."

I tried to think calmly. What would Sam do in a situation like this? He would freak out, then remember something he read about how to survive in the desert.

"What have I read about the desert? It's made of sand. It's hot. You die."

Not very Sam-like, I thought. I started walking in circles.

What would Fred do? He would hit us both with his hat and tell us to start walking.

I didn't have a hat. So I hit myself on the side of the head and said, "Come on. It's not going to do us any good to walk in circles. Get to the top of that sand dune." I pointed to the top of the nearest sand dune ... and followed my directions.

The hot sun beat down on me. The hot sand shifted under my bare feet. I fell. I crawled. I talked to myself some more.

"Keep moving," I said. "Pull yourself together."

I finally made it to the top of the dune.

"See?" I said. "We did it. And look—"

I looked.

"More . . . uh . . . sand.

"I told you it wouldn't help," I said.

"You did not," I said.

"I did too," I said.

"Did not.

"Did too. Did not. Did too."

I knocked myself down and started wrestling myself.

I won.

I looked up into the hot blue sky. Something circled overhead. Probably vultures.

"Marco?" I called.

"Polo," I answered.

"Marco . . . ?"

Nothing but the hot dry wind.

"Marco . . . ?"

I don't know how long I lay there.

I saw dancing lines of glasses of water. I saw Sam and Fred splashing in a pool.

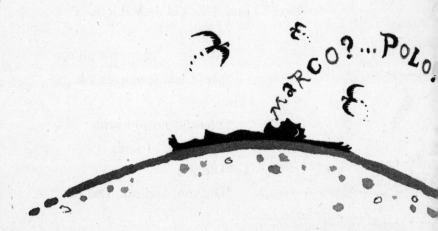

I cupped my hands to my mouth and yelled some more:

"MARCO . . . POLO! MARCO . . . POLO! MARCO . . . POLO!"

This was it, I decided. The end of the Time Warp Trio. And how weird and wrong that there was only one of the trio.

"Sam . . . Fred . . . Marco . . . Polo . . ." I croaked.

Everything went suddenly dark.

I smelled something horrible. Death?

I kept my eyes closed.

I didn't want to cheat.

I croaked, "Marco . . ."

Someone answered, "Polo."

I lifted my arms and felt blindly. I grabbed something.

I opened my eyes.

I was holding the leg of a real, live, incredibly gross-smelling camel.

"Marco Polo?" I asked.

A young man wearing a long brownish

robe and a blue turban looked down at me from his saddle on the camel.

"No, that's my camel. I am Marco Polo. But who are you? And what are you doing lying in the middle of the desert in nothing but your red underwear?"

四

"Marco Polo, I am so glad to see you," I said. "See—my name is Joe. I'm not really from around here. I warped here by accident. Now I just need to find *The Book* to get back home. And this is not my underwear. It's my swimsuit."

Marco Polo looked at me like I was from Mars.

He made his camel kneel down, and he hopped off.

"Here," he said. "Drink some water. I think the sun has cooked your brain."

I drank from his water skin. It was the best drink ever.

"You are Marco Polo, the famous explorer, aren't you?" I said. "You look kind of young to have been exploring for twenty-four years."

The young guy in the long robe and turban looked at me. "Yes, I am Marco Polo. But how do you know about me?" He suddenly pulled a long curved sword out of his robe. He held the sharp point against my bare chest.

"Are you a spy? Sent by my father and my uncle?"

I put my hands up. Now I was really in trouble. How was I going to explain time-warping and the future and how I knew about it . . . without sounding like a nut?

"Well," I said. "I know all that . . . from my horoscope," I said.

Marco look surprised. "What? You are an astrologer?"

The tip of the sword poked my chest. "Ow. I mean—yes," I lied. "And if you put that sword away, I can tell you much more."

Marco thought about it for a second. Then he put his knife back in his robe. He gave me a robe to wear, and showed me how to wrap a turban around my head. Then I tried to remember everything Sam had said about Marco Polo.

We sat next to each other, sheltered from the wind by the sitting camel.

"You have traveled all the way from Italy," I said.

"Yes," said Marco.

"You have seen many strange and wonderful things," I said.

"Oh yes," said Marco.

"You will spend twenty-four years exploring all of Asia, and then return to Italy to tell everyone about your travels," I said.

"Oh no I won't," said Marco. "I just turned twenty-one, and I'm not going to spend the best years of my life wandering around nowhere like this."

"But . . . but . . . you have to," I said. "Otherwise, how are you going to be famous for exploring China? And how will kids play Marco Polo in pools everywhere? And do you happen to have a thin blue *Book* with silver designs?"

Marco handed me the water skin. "You are as bad as my father and my uncle. That's all they talk about. Going to China. Going to see Kublai Khan. It has taken us three years to get here from Italy. When I heard the desert calling my name, I knew I should leave the caravan and go back to Italy on my own."

The late afternoon sun beat down on us. Sand swirled over our feet.

I had a bad feeling I had really messed something up.

"You heard the desert calling your name?" I said.

"Yes," said Marco.

"So you decided to leave your dad's caravan?"

"Yes," said Marco.

"Oh boy," I said. "Sam is going to kill me if he ever finds out I messed up history this bad. Maybe we should go talk this over with your dad and uncle."

Marco looked out over the endless sand dunes. "It's no use. They love this stuff. They are crazy merchants. They spent three years dodging bandits and sandstorms and pirates and robbers. For what? To bring metal and ivory and glass to trade for spices and silk?"

"That does sound a little crazy," I said. "Especially since you don't have any cars or trains or jets."

Marco went on. "I have not heard of cars or trains or jets. But I have seen many strange sights. In Persia we saw people who worshipped fire. They had a cloth you could put in the fire and pull out unharmed. Birds and animals no one from Italy has ever seen. Fantastic. But I miss home. I miss the water everywhere in Venice. I miss the food, my friends."

"Me too," I said. "And you know what? If we find this blue *Book* I'm looking for, I can get us both home . . . in a lot less than three years."

"I don't have such a thing," said Marco. "But my father has talked about a book exactly like this."

"What? Are you kidding?" I said. "What are we waiting for? Let's get out of this sandbox and find your dad."

Marco looked up and scanned a dark cloud over the sand dunes.

"Yes," said Marco. "We should go now."

We climbed up on Marco's camel. Marco sat between the two shaggy humps on its back. I sat behind the back hump and hung on as the camel lurched to its feet. We swayed side to side as the camel started walking.

"This is great," I said. "I'm glad you decided to go back and talk to your dad. As an astrologer, I can see that this is all going to work out fine."

Marco turned around to

22

look at me. Then he looked again at the dark cloud approaching us. "It is time to go because that cloud is a sandstorm with a gang of bandits riding in front of it."

"What?" I squeaked.

"If the bandits catch us, they will either sell us into slavery or just kill us. If we get caught in the sandstorm, we will be buried alive. But I am not worried."

Our camel started to trot.

I felt like my eyeballs were going to be jolted out of my head. "Why are you not worried?" I said.

"Because you are a famous astrologer, Joe. And you said everything would work out fine."

五

Riding a walking camel feels like riding a small boat bobbing in the ocean.

Riding a running camel feels like riding a hairy jackhammer.

Our camel huffed and galloped and snorted along the top of a sand dune. I held on to its shaggy, smelly back hump.

The bandits' yells and screams grew louder.

A hot wind blasted my back with sand.

I looked back. The bandits were closing in.

Our camel ran.

I bounced.

The wind blew.

The bandits pulled closer.

"Can't this thing go any faster?" I yelled. "The planets tell me that we should go faster . . . or we will become bandit roadkill."

Marco pulled the reins to one side. Our camel turned and started sliding down the side of the mountain of sand. I fell forward. My turban smashed down over my eyes.

"Marco!" I yelled.

"Polo!" Marco yelled back.

"No, Marco—" I yelled.

"Polo!" Marco yelled back. He laughed. "Now I see how you play the game, Joe Astrologer."

I bounced blindly on the camel's back. I tried to hold on with one hand and push my turban up with the other.

"No," I yelled into the swirling wind. "I . . . can't . . . see. . . ."

The sudden wind whipped the turban scarf around my face. Blowing sand stung my legs. I could hear the shouts of the bandits behind us.

"Marco," I moaned.

"Polo!" yelled Marco.

"Oh, forget it," I said.

I felt us stop sliding and start trotting again. I hung on to the bouncing camel hump as hard as I could. Suddenly we were falling. We sailed through the air and landed in a giant pile of camel, Marco Polo, and me.

I pushed back my turban to find a shocking sight.

The bandits were gone, but so was everything else. We were swallowed up by a swirling, stinging, howling, bury-you-alive sandstorm.

Marco and I huddled behind the sitting camel. It

had its eyes and even its nose closed tight against the blowing sand.

"Joe Astrologer, you were right," yelled Marco. "No more bandits."

"Great," I yelled back.

But as I wrapped my turban around my face, I was just a little bit worried about being lost, not ever finding *The Book*, not ever getting home, and being buried alive.

六

The sun disappeared and took every bit of light with it.

Now we were sunk in a wind-howling, sand-blasting, camel-funk-smelling blackness. There was nothing else. No way to fight it. Nothing to do but keep my head down and try to breathe.

I nodded off. I woke up to feel sand piling over my feet. I shook it off. We were getting buried alive.

The night seemed to last forever. Sand. Wind. Dark. Shaking off sand.

I drifted in and out of sleep. I dreamed of sand blowing over me. I dreamed of the sand covering me completely.

I was looking at where I used to be. It wasn't there anymore. The only thing there was:

I remember thinking how funny that would be to read in a book.

If you had to read a whole chapter for an assignment, you could just read that little bit at the beginning, look at the empty sandstorm pages, and then you would be done with a chapter.

"Joe."

A voice called to me in my sand-buried dream.

"Joe Astrologer."

The voice wouldn't go away. Didn't it know I was buried alive?

"Joe Astrologer—look."

Now the voice was grabbing me and shaking my shoulder.

I opened my sand-crusted eyes. I could see! I wasn't buried alive. I was unburied alive.

The wind had stopped. The sandblasting had stopped. The face of Marco Polo looked down at me.

"Look, Joe Astrologer." Marco pointed behind our still-sitting camel, half buried in a sand drift.

"Wuhh," I said, with a dry mouth crunching bits of sand.

"That's right," said Marco Polo. "A wall."

"Wonderful," I said. "A wall." I didn't get it.

"It all worked out fine," said Marco Polo. "Just like you said it would. We found the oasis."

We walked into a grove of palm trees. A stream of water fell through rocks into a pool. A pool of beautiful water. Men in robes and turbans loaded boxes and bags onto camels sitting under palm trees.

I couldn't believe we had been that close to the oasis and never seen it. That was some blinding sandstorm.

Two men in robes and turbans ran toward us.

"Uh-oh," I said. I knew our good luck couldn't hold. I got ready to run.

Marco held me by my robe. "Everything will be fine," he said.

"I wish you would stop saying that," I said.

The two men ran up to us and wrapped Marco in a giant hug.

"Marco," said the first man.

"We were so worried about you," said the second man.

Marco smiled at me. "Astrologer Joe, meet my father Niccolò Polo, and my uncle Maffeo Polo. Joe saved me from bandits and the sandstorm, and he found the oasis."

Niccolò and Maffeo squeezed me in a giant hug.

"Fantastic," they said.

"Amazing," they said.

"It was nothing," I said. "I mean it. Really. I'm not kidding."

"Anything you want is yours," said Marco Polo's dad. "Pick whatever you would wish from our caravan. Gold, steel, glass, rubies. It is yours."

I looked at the long line of camels loaded with all kinds of treasures.

"You know what I would really like?" I said.

"Anything," said Marco's uncle.

"A thin blue *Book* with silver designs."

Marco's dad looked at Marco. He looked at Marco's uncle. He looked back at me.

"A thin blue book with silver designs?" he asked.

I nodded.

"With silver writing from strange languages?" he asked.

"Yes," I said.

"With strange pictures inside?"

"Yes, yes," I almost shouted.

"We don't have it," said Marco Polo's dad.

"But—" I said.

"But we have seen a book just like that at the court of Kublai Khan," said Marco's uncle. "We are heading to see him. You must join us."

I sat down right there in the sand. I was stuck. No *Book*. And no choice but to stay and join the Polo family.

"I wish Sam and Fred were here."

Niccolò looked at Maffeo.

"I know, I know," I said. "You don't have such a thing."

"Would this Sam be a little scrawny one with round pieces of glass wired on his head?" said Niccolò.

"And would this Fred be wearing a strange hat with a piece that sticks out in front?" said Uncle Maffeo.

"What?" I said. "I mean yes. I mean have you seen them?"

"We bought them from some bandits yesterday," said Niccolò. "The scrawny one talked us into the deal. He said he knew everything about the great Khan who we are going to see. The one with the hat said he could tell the future."

"We got them in a trade for a sick camel," said Uncle Maffeo. "I think we got cheated."

"We were planning to leave them here," added Niccolò.

"Here?" I said. "Sam and Fred are here?"

Niccolò and Maffeo both pointed to a pool on the other side of the oasis. There was a kid in a black swimsuit splashing another kid in an awful yellow suit.

"Sam!" I shouted.

I couldn't believe I had found Sam and Fred.

Sam and Fred couldn't believe they had found me.

While everyone else in the caravan packed up the camels and horses, Fred and Sam and I filled each other in.

Sam told the whole story of how he saw the green mist leak out of my backpack and time-warp us out of the YMCA pool when we starting playing Marco Polo.

Fred added details about getting caught by bandits and being sold to the Polos.

I told the story of me bravely fighting off the bandits, cleverly surviving the sandstorm, and finding the oasis.

"Yeah, right," said Fred.

And then it was time to go.

The camel master of the caravan piled all three of us on one sitting camel. The camel rocked to its feet.

We fell forward, backward, left, and right. Then we were on the way out of the oasis in a dusty line of camels, horses, and men.

"I know we should be glad they didn't leave us back there," said Sam in front of me. "But I am seriously going to yack if this camel doesn't smooth out."

"What are you complaining about?" said Fred behind me. "I got the back row here, and it smells like—"

"It is so good to be back with you guys," I said. "Look at us—robes, turbans, camel. We are the real thing."

"Are we there yet?" said Fred. "I'm hungry."

"And where the heck is *The Book* this time?" said Sam. "I've got to get back to Brooklyn for my piano lesson."

"Some things never change," I said.

The caravan snaked through the desert, toward soaring mountains in front of us. Soon the land around us changed to small clumps of grass and low bushes. Everything turned greener as we got closer to the mountain.

Someone riding a sturdy brown horse rode up next to our camel.

"Marco," I said.

"Polo," he answered automatically. He rode alongside us. "Joe Astrologer, I want to thank you for changing my life. Now that I know everything is going to be fine, I feel like I could explore the whole world."

Fred and Sam gave me a weird look.

"And now we are just two days away from the summer palace of the Great Khan. What do the stars tell you about our meeting, Joe Astrologer?"

"Well . . ." I said. I looked around the clear blue sky. "I'll have to check with the stars later. Let me do that and get back to you."

Marco waved. "Excellent, Joe Astrologer. I told my uncle it was worth it to keep you and your crazy friends. We'll talk later." He nudged his horse and galloped back toward the front of the caravan. He turned and waved. "Marco!"

"Polo," I answered.

We rolled along silently on our camel for a bit.

"Joe Astrologer?" said Sam.

"The Great Con?" said Fred.

"It's kind of a long story," I said. "But Marco and his dad and his uncle think we are all astrologers."

"—and we are going to meet a great convict?" said Fred.

"No, no, no," said Sam. "That's Khan with a K, not Con with a C. He's Kublai Khan, the grandson of Genghis Khan, the guy who conquered half of the world over here."

"And he's got *The Book*," I said.

"So we must be in China," said Sam. "Sometime around twelve seventy."

"Yeah, that's what I thought," said Fred.

"So let me guess," I said. "This Kublai Khan is a crazy maniac who chops the heads off astrologers and feeds them to his wild dogs just for fun."

I rolled along on our camel and thought about that terrible idea. Suddenly the grass didn't look so green anymore. And the sky didn't look so blue.

"No," said Sam. "Not at all. And that's the strange thing. Kublai Khan was a very smart and good ruler. He was a Mongol warrior who conquered most of China. But he was interested in learning about all different parts of the world. He's most famous for being crazy rich and building his amazing summer palace—Xanadu."

40

"What's so strange about that?" said Fred.

"The strange part is that I can't remember *The Book* ever warping us into someplace nice," said Sam. "It makes sense that we are on the Silk Road in China with Marco Polo. And *The Book* is probably somewhere in the summer palace at Xanadu. But what could be dangerous about hanging out with a nice, rich guy?"

We flopped back and forth on our strolling camel.

"Maybe our time-warp luck is finally changing," said Fred.

"Maybe we're actually getting good at time-warping," I said.

"I doubt it, and I don't think so," said Sam.

Our caravan cut through a pass in the mountains and came out on beautiful green fields. We were riding with Marco Polo, heading toward meeting Kublai Khan at his famous palace at Xanadu.

I wondered what my horoscope for tomorrow might say.

Then I remembered I was the guy who was supposed to come up with a horoscope for tomorrow.

九

Like all caravans along the Silk Road, we traveled in a large group for safety. The people in the towns protected the caravans because they wanted to trade with them. It was the bandits and robbers in between the towns you had to watch out for.

We changed our camels for horses. We slept in tents made of animal skins. We ate the strangest collection of dried fruits and odd stews. But we didn't care. Each day brought us closer to Xanadu, and closer to *The Book*.

The night before we were to finally meet Kublai Khan, Fred, Sam, and I sat around the night campfire with Marco Polo, his dad, and his uncle. Everyone was looking at me.

"So tell us, Joe Astrologer," said Uncle Maffeo, "what do you see for tomorrow?"

I looked around the campfire. I drew some lines in the dirt with a stick . . . and hoped they looked like astrology kind of lines.

43

"Well, I see partly cloudy skies with a chance of time travel."

The Polo family looked confused.

I suddenly saw the future. And it looked like a lot of people being very mad at a fake astrologer.

"Kidding," I said. "I'm just kidding. That's a thing we do with horoscopes in our land—Brooklyn. First we kid. Then we get right down to business."

Marco Polo nodded.

Sam covered his eyes with his hands.

Fred ate the last of the fire-roasted bird on a stick we had for dinner.

The campfire flickered on everyone's faces. I looked up and noticed an amazing blanket of stars. They were beautiful against the deep blue-black sky. But they weren't telling me anything new. I took a deep breath and started talking.

"As you know, astrology is a very tricky thing. The planets spin, stars move around, some people see pictures they make—"

"What about Kublai Khan?" said Uncle Maffeo. "It has been eight years since we last saw him. Will he welcome us?"

"Or have things changed?" said Father Niccolò.

"You know what another great magician . . . I mean astrologer, my uncle Joe says: the more things change, the more things stay the same."

The Polos thought about this for a second. They nodded their heads. I kept talking.

"Kublai Khan is a very smart and very good ruler. For tomorrow I see a most amazing summer palace. Beautiful. Rich. Really over the top. A crazy rich good ruler."

This is what everyone wanted to hear. I could see the excitement in all of their faces.

The fire popped and sent sparks rushing up to the starry night sky. I was on a good roll. I really got into it.

"And I see fancy silk robes, jewels, parties, dragons, pepperoni pizza!"

I looked over at Sam. He was making the classic slicing motion with his finger that means *cut.* Cut it out *now.*

I looked back at the Polo family. They were looking a little confused.

"Oh," I said. "And so to wrap it all up, our horoscope for tomorrow is: You will meet an old friend. But be careful. Sometimes when life looks best, things get worse."

And I said it like I really meant it. Because that is the truth Fred and Sam and I have learned every time we have ever time-warped.

"Yes," said Marco Polo's dad. "How true."

Uncle Maffeo nodded.

Marco smiled.

Fred licked the bird-roasting stick.

"And as soon as someone finds a thin blue *Book* with silver designs," I added, "they should bring it to an official astrologer."

Smoke and sparks rose to the stars.

"And don't forget to wear your hat and sunscreen."

"**D**on't forget to wear your hat and sunscreen?" said Sam.

It was morning. The remaining horses carried the caravan goods. Now we walked. We were headed to our meeting with the head of the Mongols, conqueror of a good chunk of China, and ruler of everything around—Kublai Khan.

"I got a little carried away," I said.

Fred laughed. "Parties, dragons, and pepperoni pizza?"

"Hey, I didn't see you guys helping out," I said.

"Ugh," said Sam, trudging along the dirt road. "I never thought I'd say this, but I miss our camel."

"Maybe we can help the Chinese invent taxis," said Fred.

"I don't think the Chinese people need your help inventing things," said Sam. "Even now in twelve seventy-five they already invented gunpowder, wheelbarrows, umbrellas, and paperback books hundreds of years ago."

We walked in the giant caravan of horses and mules loaded with bags. The people we saw along the road looked different now. Dark hair. Beardless faces. We saw deer and pheasant in the woods. A big beast with horns pulling a plow.

"Yak," said Sam.

"Are you getting sick again?" said Fred.

"That's the name of the beast pulling the plow," said Sam.

Marco still had his horse and rode it back along the road to find us in the middle of the caravan.

"Marco!" said Fred.

"Polo!" answered Marco.

"Can we please stop that now?" said Sam.

"Good news," said Marco. "The Khan is eager to see us. You are very good, Joe Astrologer."

Marco turned his horse and galloped off.

I smiled. "Boys, I think our fortunes are changing," I said.

And boy, was I ever right . . . and wrong.

The farming countryside slowly gave way to small mud houses. The mud houses became a city of buildings with reddish tile roofs. Groups of Chinese men, women, and children began to line the roads and look at us. Fred waved and tipped his cap. The little kids smiled.

Before we knew it, we were at the tall stone-and-earth walls surrounding Kublai Khan's palace.

Marco Polo rode back and escorted us to the front.

"Our caravan will camp out here," said Marco. "But the Khan has sent word that he wants to see us now. I asked my father and uncle if you could accompany us. They said yes—as long as the two goofy ones don't say anything."

"Hey," said Fred. "Who is he calling 'goofy ones'?"

Sam rolled his eyes. "Two guesses. And the first one doesn't count."

I put my hand over Fred's mouth so he wouldn't say anything else. "We would be honored," I said.

Marco handed us clean robes. "Put these on. Then meet us at the gate." He rode off to get ready himself.

I let Fred loose.

"Goofy ones—right. I'll show them. I'm not going," said Fred.

Sam took off his dusty traveling robe. One of the caravan guys pointed at his bright yellow swimsuit and laughed.

"Come on, Fred, we have to find *The Book*."

"No way," said Fred.

"It's our only chance to get home," I said, putting on

my new robe. The same guy laughed at my red swimsuit.

"Not a chance," said Fred.

"They will have all kinds of food," I said.

"Really?" said Fred.

"Definitely," said Sam.

"Okay," said Fred. "Just this once I'll let it slide, and give them another chance."

We all got into our robes and met the Polos at the gate.

Marco and his dad and his uncle were all decked out in their best clothes from back home in Italy. They wore long fancy robes and pointed shoes. Maffeo and Niccolò both wore heavy gold chains around their necks.

"Whoa," said Fred. "You guys are looking sharp. Nice duds."

The giant wooden gates—covered in carvings of birds, fish, and every kind of

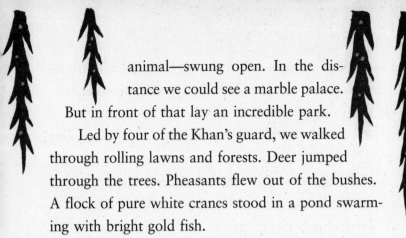

animal—swung open. In the distance we could see a marble palace.
But in front of that lay an incredible park.

Led by four of the Khan's guard, we walked
through rolling lawns and forests. Deer jumped
through the trees. Pheasants flew out of the bushes.
A flock of pure white cranes stood in a pond swarm-
ing with bright gold fish.

All of us, even Sam, were speechless.

We approached a giant open-air tent kind of thing
in front of the palace. Tall red columns carved in the
shape of dragons held up a roof of gold-covered bam-
boo. White silk cords anchored each column. Rows
and rows of covered tables surrounded with pillows
filled the space. Rows and rows of palace visitors sat
waiting. Every one of them watched
our every move

"Yikes," said Sam.

The guards led us to the

head of the tables, just below a gigantic golden throne. They motioned for us to bow down with our foreheads on the ground.

We stayed like that for probably five minutes, but it seemed like forever.

"All right already," whispered Fred. "That's about enough of this. Let's get this show on the road."

Fred started to get up.

Sam and I held him down.

"It might be hard to find *The Book* if we're dead," I whispered.

There was a loud gong. Everyone looked up.

And there was a man with dark hair and sparkling black eyes standing in front of the throne. The ruler of empires. The boss of millions. Kublai Khan.

"Rise," he said. "Welcome back, Niccolò and Maffeo. Tell me everything about your journey."

Marco's dad and uncle told the Khan stories of bandits, sandstorms, and strange people. They gave him letters and gifts. I thought they had completely forgotten about us.

"And who is this fellow?" said the Khan.

Fred started to introduce himself. I covered his mouth again.

"My son," said Niccolò.

"He is welcome here," said Kublai Khan.

At that, all the people at the tables clapped and cheered.

We were in. It was good.

The Khan's servants directed the Polos and Fred and Sam and me to seats of honor just below the Khan's table. He waved a hand and said, "Welcome to our guests from distant lands. Now let us begin the feast to honor them."

Marco smiled at me. Everything was fine for him.

Fred smiled at the steaming platter of roast duck headed his way.

We were safely in Xanadu.

Now all we had to do was find *The Book*.

What could go wrong?

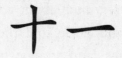

If anyone ever asks you about Kublai Khan, tell them that he throws a great party. Endless bowls of duck, fish, noodles, soups, vegetables, and cakes covered our table. Acrobats, dancers, and jugglers entertained the hundreds of guests.

Kublai Khan was definitely the boss. Every time he lifted his cup to drink, everyone (including us) had to kneel and bow down. Musicians played a little song until he set his cup back down. Then everyone would get up and start eating and talking again.

"Now that is respect," said Fred, slurping another mouthful of noodles.

Marco Polo chewed a small cake. "He is a leader who has earned respect. He is the most powerful man in this part of the world."

I looked at the great Kublai Khan in his gold robe. He lifted his cup to drink.

Everyone knelt and bowed.

The Khan's royal music played.

He set his cup down.

Everyone got up and started eating and talking again.

That's when I figured it out.

"This is one powerful guy," I said. "So how do we ask him for *The Book*?"

"Oh I'm sure we could just walk up and ask him," said Sam.

Fred finished his bowl of noodles with a large slurp. "Sounds good to me."

"Fred, I was kidding," said Sam.

"What have we got to lose?" said Fred.

"Oh, maybe just our heads, our lives—the usual," said Sam. "You know how things always go wrong when we are time-warping. I say we stay low. Don't draw too much attention to ourselves."

A small man with beady eyes appeared at our table. He gave a little bow and said, "The great Khan wishes to speak with all of you."

"So much for staying low," said Sam.

The small guy led us up to the Khan's table. We sat on four big cushions down in front of the Khan. Marco Polo's dad and uncle sat at the table just below the Khan, so their heads were even with his feet.

Kublai Khan looked us over. "Welcome, son of Niccolò," he said to Marco. "I understand from your father that you are interested in many things."

Marco nodded. "Yes, great Khan. We have seen so many amazing sights on our trip already. And my father tells me that the wonders of your kingdom are the most amazing of all."

Kublai Khan smiled a big smile that lit up his whole face. "I can show you many wonders: exploding powder that can shoot a missile the length of a city, giant kites that can lift a man into the air—"

"How about a thin blue *Book* with silver designs?" Fred blurted out.

Everyone froze.

"What?" said Kublai Khan, looking down at us. He did not look happy to be interrupted.

Sam put his hands on his head. "I knew it. We're dead."

A dangerous couple of seconds of silence ticked by. Then Marco Polo saved the day.

"I'm sorry, great Khan," said Marco. "I forgot to introduce you to three astrologers from the far nation called Brook-Land. They have also heard much about you and wanted to meet you. They are Joe, Sam, and Fred."

I bowed. Sam bowed. Fred waved.

Kublai Khan sat forward. "Astrologers? From Brook-Land? Interesting. What method do you use to see the future?"

Sam looked at me.

Fred looked at me.

I guessed it was up to me to answer.

"Well, your great Khan, sir," I said. "In our land we usually read our horoscopes in the paper every day."

"Interesting," said Kublai Khan. "Our astrologers follow the moon, but they also write daily books. You must meet my new Royal Astrologer."

The small beady-eyed guy who had led us up to the table stood at Kublai Khan's side.

"Very pleased to meet you," said the Royal Astrologer.

But he didn't look at all pleased. In fact, he looked downright mad at us. I guess we were his competition.

"Oh no," said Sam. "I knew it. Don't tell me. You are mad that we might take over your job. And now you are working on some nasty plan to get rid of us so we are never heard from ever again."

The beady-eyed little guy looked shocked. Like Sam had read his mind.

Then he went back to his fake smile. "Oh no," he said. "We astrologers must share what we know. If you are astrologers . . . what animal sign rules your birth?"

If this was a test, I was flunking it already. I had no idea what he was talking about.

"Animal sign?" I repeated to stall for time.

"Yes," said the Royal Astrologer.

"Certainly," said Kublai Khan.

The Astrologer was setting me up to look stupid.

"Well . . ." I said.

"Dog," said Sam. "We were all born in the Year of the Dog. We are fiercely loyal and protect our friends no matter what."

The Royal Astrologer looked surprised again. "Oh. You know our astrology?"

"Absolutely," said Sam. He adjusted his glasses. "Based on the twelve animals that visited the Buddha. Each animal rules a different year."

Fred and I stared at Sam. We were just as surprised as the Royal Astrologer was. We had no idea Sam knew about Chinese astrology.

"Well, of course," said the Royal Astrologer. "Everyone knows that. Tell me something I don't know."

This guy was such a weasel. I decided to use an old Uncle Joe trick to show him up. It was probably not the best idea for making friends. But it sure felt good.

"We can also predict things," I said.

"Oh really?" said the Royal Astrologer.

"What can you predict?" said Kublai Khan.

"I will predict what the Royal Astrologer is going to

say," I said. I walked over to Kublai Khan and whispered in his ear, "Sixty-eight."

Then I said to the Royal Astrologer, "Pick a number between fifty and one hundred where both digits are even, and they are different from each other."

The Royal Astrologer thought for a second. Now he knew I was trying to show him up. He said, "Sixty-eight."

"Amazing," said Kublai Khan. "Just as you had predicted."

I bowed.

The Royal Astrologer looked completely mad.

He had no idea how I did it. But the trick is pretty simple. With that set of rules to pick a number, people will almost always pick 68.

"Very good," said the Royal Astrologer. He gave me that fake smile of his and said, "But remember, there is only one Royal Astrologer. And that is me—Ding . . ."

The more some things change, the more they stay the same.

I knew he was going to tell us his last name.

And I knew what it was going to be.

And I knew we were about to get into even more trouble.

" . . . Dong," he said. "Never forget—Ding Dong."

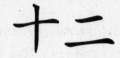

If you know me and Fred and Sam, you know that in our time-warp travels we have had some trouble with bad guys. Often we have had trouble because these bad guys have bad names. Really bad names.

But—Ding Dong? Was he kidding?

No, he was not.

Ding Dong stared at all three of us. It was like he was daring us to laugh.

I bit my lip.

Fred held his breath.

Sam covered his own mouth.

We did not laugh.

Ding Dong turned to Kublai Khan. "I must leave now and prepare for the hunt tomorrow. If you wish, I will be glad to take care of these three . . . astrologers tomorrow."

"An excellent idea," said Kublai Khan. "Thank you, Astrologer Ding."

Ding Dong bowed once more. Then he left without giving us another look.

Kublai Khan turned back to Marco Polo. "Tomorrow we shall have a great hunt in honor of our visitors."

Marco Polo's dad raised his cup to Kublai Khan. Everyone cheered and bowed and smiled.

Fred and Sam and I got up to leave.

"Oh yes," said Kublai Khan. "And the blue book? With silver designs?"

We froze. We thought we were in trouble again.

"You must get the Royal Astrologer to show it to you. He tells me it is one of the most valuable books in my collection."

We couldn't believe what we had just heard.

"The Royal Astrologer?" said Sam.

"Has *The Book*?" said Fred.

"With twisting silver designs?" I said.

Kublai Khan stood up and stretched out his arms. His big gold robe made him look like a giant bird. "Yes, yes, yes," he said.

"Ding Dong," I said. But this time it wasn't funny. Because now we realized that the one guy who had just become our biggest enemy was holding our ticket home.

"By the way, what happened to the old Royal Astrologer?" I said.

"Hunting accident," said Kublai Khan.

Then I felt even worse.

Ding. Dong.

十三

Ding Dong had, of course, disappeared. We couldn't find him anywhere. So we couldn't find *The Book* anywhere either.

There was nothing we could do except finish the Khan's giant party. The party went on forever. More food. More drinks. Acrobats, speeches, music. We were asleep on our feet by the time the Polos led us back to the caravan.

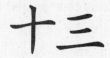

We fell into a tent and slept like logs. It seemed like only five minutes later that Marco Polo was waking us up and hustling us back to the Khan's palace to be ready to meet him for hunting at dawn.

We stood outside the red-roofed palace, still half asleep.

"Urg," said Fred. "Where am I?"

"Kublai Khan's summer palace at Xanadu. In the year twelve seventy-five," said Sam. "With your chances of ever seeing your home in Brooklyn looking slim to none." Sam did not look happy.

"But we've got a plan," I said. "We'll meet up with Ding Dong today. We'll be nice to him. We'll get *The Book* and warp out of here."

"Mrrghf," said Sam. Sam is not a morning person.

Then the Khan showed up for the hunt. And when the Khan shows up, he really shows up.

Two giant wooden doors to the stable swung open. One thousand big black hunting dogs came spilling out, led on leashes by guys in blue outfits. Then another thousand brown hunting dogs followed, held on leashes by guys in deep red outfits.

Horns trumpeted as the morning sky turned from pink to yellow.

Three hundred all-white horses trotted out. Some horsemen carried hawks tied to their wrists. Other hunters rode with giant cats on leashes behind them.

"What the heck?" said Fred.

"Kublai Khan loves his white horses," said Marco Polo. "The horse is what carried him and his Mongol warriors all over Asia. The horse made him ruler of all the East."

67

"Yeah, I'm sure," said Fred. "But what's with the birds and cats?"

"Hunting hawks," said Marco. "They are trained to hunt small animals like rabbits and other birds. The leopards and lynxes are trained to hunt the bigger animals like wild pigs, bulls, and deer."

Rows of white horses trotted past us.

One of the trained leopards growled at us. We got a very close and scary look at his large, sharp teeth.

"I'm glad he's on our side," said Fred.

Drums beat. Cymbals crashed.

Then a very impressive elephant clomped slowly out of the gates. It wore a jeweled headband, tigerskins draped across its back, and a little white house covered by a golden umbrella on top of that.

The hunters cheered. Hounds barked. The sun rose. A man dressed all in gold waved from atop the elephant. It was Kublai Khan.

"What the heck is an elephant doing in China?" said Sam.

"A special gift to the Khan from the south," said Marco. "The Khan has many elephants. He rides them in comfort to the hunting grounds. Then he rides his horses to hunt."

"I like his style," said Fred

We were still standing there, hypnotized by the

crazy sight of it all, when one of the horsemen rode up to us.

"Astrologers, your horses," said the rider.

"Ding Dong," said Fred. "We've been looking for you."

"We need that blue *Book*," said Sam. He wasn't messing around.

Ding Dong smiled. He pulled a thin blue book from his saddle bag. "This one?"

It was *The Book*. We were saved.

"Yes," I almost shouted.

"But of course," said Ding Dong. "As soon as we finish the hunt."

"I knew it was too good to be true," said Sam.

"Oh, come on," said Fred. "Let's enjoy ourselves. We've found *The Book*. Let's ride some horses and do some hunting."

I would rather have grabbed *The Book* and warped safely home right then. But we didn't have much choice.

Ding Dong put *The Book* back into his bag and motioned to his men to help us up on the three horses behind him.

The parade of dogs, hunters, hawks, horses, cats, and the Khan's elephant marched off toward the palace walls.

"I'll travel with Father and meet you at the hunt," said Marco Polo. "You astrologers must have plenty of secrets to discuss." He rode off toward the parade of hunters.

Fred, Sam, and I got on the horses behind Ding Dong.

"I should probably tell you—we don't usually ride horses back in our land," I said.

"No?" said Ding Dong. "What do you ride?"

"Skateboards and subways," said Fred.

Ding Dong had no idea what we were talking about. But he smiled anyway. Not a good sign.

十四

"Hold on then," said Ding Dong. "We will take a special shortcut to the hunting grounds."

Ding Dong took off on his horse, heading away from the main hunting parade. Our horses followed right behind. We sort of rode, but mostly just hung on.

We hung on out of the palace grounds. We hung on through the surrounding village. We hung on over the dirt road that turned into a path, that crossed the fields, that turned into the woods.

Ding Dong led us deep into the woods. Our four horses scared up birds from the bushes. Small deer jumped from behind trees.

Sam squeezed his horse's neck, looking like he was going to throw up.

Fred held his horse's reins in one hand, looking like he knew what he was doing.

Then Ding Dong suddenly stopped. He jumped off

his horse. We were glad to slide down off our horses.

"Oh, my aching butt," said Sam.

"That was great," said Fred.

"Where is everybody else?" I said.

Ding Dong smiled. "Oh, they'll be here later. Too late for you."

I had a feeling we might be in trouble when three guys in black outfits suddenly appeared from behind the trees.

I knew we were in trouble when they jumped on our horses and rode off.

We turned back to see Ding Dong holding the leashes of three of the hunting leopards we had seen earlier that morning.

"Well, astrologers," he said, "can you predict your future horoscope now?"

I saw a bad news future, but I didn't want to believe it. I tried to think of a plan.

"Let us see *The Book* and we'll tell you a great horoscope," I said.

Ding Dong pulled *The Book* out of his loose robe.

"No. Let me tell you tell you your horoscope without even looking." One of the big cats on the leash growled and jumped at us. "Hunting can be very dangerous," said Ding Dong. "Especially when the hunters become the hunted."

He laughed.

Fred and Sam and I backed against a tree.

We heard the bark of hounds, the cry of hawks—all the sounds of hunters in the distance.

Ding Dong unhooked the leopards' leashes.

"The cats are usually trained to bring down deer," said Ding Dong. "But I have trained them to take care of more human problems."

Fred, Sam, and I looked at each other.

Now our horoscope for the day was terribly clear:

We were the hunters about to become the hunted.

十五

The three leopards jumped into the clearing in front of us. They growled and twitched their tails. They looked hungry.

"I really, really do not like cats," said Sam.

"Allergies?" said Fred.

"Yeah, I'm allergic to their sharp teeth," said Sam.

The cats spread out and crept toward us. They had us covered. There was no way to escape.

"Joe, do something," said Sam.

I tried to think of a trick that might impress a giant hungry mad cat. "Does anyone have a giant ball of string?"

I had nothing. Nothing but those stupid horoscopes running through my head.

"Uh, don't forget your sunscreen?" I said.

"You are a sad excuse for astrologers," said Ding Dong. Now he was smiling for real. "Now I see I didn't need to kill you. You are too stupid to know my plan. But I thought you were reading my mind. I didn't want to take a chance."

"Well, don't kill us then," said Sam. "We don't know anything about your stupid plan."

Ding Dong pulled out a roll of papers. "You mean this plan? My plan to get rid of Kublai Khan?" said Ding Dong.

We backed against the tree as the cats got closer.

"Yeah, your plan to get rid of Kublai Khan," said Fred.

Ding Dong smiled again. "Oh, now you do know my plan. So now I will have to kill you."

Ding Dong said something to the leopards. They moved closer.

"The pen is mightier than the sword," I said, still spouting horoscopes, trying to come up with an idea. I had no idea what I was saying. But luckily for us, Fred did.

He bent down slowly, with his hands hidden behind him, and picked up two good-sized rocks. He straightened up as Ding Dong kept blabbering on.

"When I give the command, my leopards will attack. You will be the victims of an unfortunate hunting accident," said Ding Dong.

"Marco!" I called, getting desperate.

"Polo," said Sam.

The cats crouched, waiting for the word to spring . . . and turn us into Time Warp Cat Chow.

But before Ding Dong could say anything, Fred yelled the rest of his horoscope: ". . . but sometimes the rock is mightier than the pen."

Fred's pitch zipped straight for Ding Dong's head and . . . missed.

Ding Dong ducked.

"Ha," said Ding Dong. "Is that the best you've got?" He stood up. "Now, my cats—"

And just as Ding Dong was about to yell, "Attack," the bushes behind him shook. He turned his head for a second.

Fred quick-pitched another fastball. Then all heck broke loose at once.

Fred's rock beanball bonked Ding Dong on the side of his head. He dropped like a chopped-down tree.

Four of the giant black hunting dogs exploded out of the bushes. They spotted the three cats, then howled.

The cats froze. They didn't wait around for any more commands from their master. They took off running as fast as they could.

The dogs instantly forgot about hunting for Kublai Khan. They barked and howled and tore through the brush on a much older and more pressing mission—chasing cats.

Sam unwrapped his arms from his head. "I think I'm getting too old for this."

I pounded Fred on the back. "Nice pitch," I said.

Fred pulled down his hat. "Thanks for calling the signal," he said. "I can't believe those goofy horoscopes came true."

The sounds of the cat-chasing hounds faded in the distance.

Sam stood up and dusted himself off. "Now let's get *The Book* and warp out of here."

We walked over to Ding Dong, still collapsed in a heap on the ground. I rolled him over. He already had a nice lump on the side of his head from Fred's bean-

ball. I took *The Book* out of his robe pocket.

I held *The Book*. We were as good as home. Then I had a thought.

"But shouldn't we tell somebody about this? If we just disappear, Ding Dong will be free to work his plan."

I could tell Sam was dying for me to open *The Book* and warp us home out of trouble. But he nodded.

"Joe's right. If Ding Dong gets rid of Kublai Khan, Marco Polo will never go on his travels."

Fred scratched his head. "So what do we do?"

I looked around. I could hear dogs, horses, horns, the sounds of the hunt all around us. I couldn't see anything. That gave me an idea. I called, "Marco?"

We heard a horn.

Fred called, "Marco?"

We heard a horse.

Sam called, "Marco?"

A white horse crashed

through the bushes. Its rider answered, "Polo!" And it was:

Marco Polo.

Marco's pack of hunting dogs swirled around us as we explained Ding Dong's plot to Marco Polo. He didn't believe us at first, but then we showed him Ding Dong's papers.

"This is terrible," said Marco Polo.

"Ah, we had it under control," said Fred, patting the dogs. One of the dogs licked Fred's face. "Us dog-guys stick together, you know?"

Marco Polo tied up Ding Dong with a rope from his horse.

"I'll get this news to Kublai Khan right away," said Marco Polo.

"And then I predict you will travel and see all kinds

of amazing things and go back home to Italy and find someone to write about your travels and become famous in swimming pools everywhere," said Sam.

"Is that my horoscope?" said Marco Polo.

"Absolutely," I said. "And everything will work out fine." Then I motioned to Sam and Fred. "Come on, guys. We've got a green mist to catch."

We hiked off into the woods so we wouldn't freak out Marco Polo (and maybe get him into trouble describing how he saw three guys disappear in a swirling green mist).

When we were out of sight, I held out *The Book*. It fell open to a page showing the Chinese zodiac of all twelve animals.

I read the entry under the Year of the Dog.

"Loyal friends, together forever. Home is where that heart is."

A pale green mist in the shape of a dog jumped out of *The Book*. It ran around us, growing bigger and bigger.

I called out, "See you later, Marco."

We couldn't see anything in the swirling dog green mist.

But we heard a faint, "Polo."

And then we were doggone.

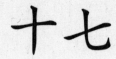

Splash.

Water.

The smell of chlorine.

We were back in the YMCA pool in Brooklyn, exactly when and where we had left.

I almost called the first name of a famous explorer. Then I thought I'd better not. No telling how a certain blue *Book* with silver designs might react.

I opened my eyes.

There was Fred, still wearing his black swimsuit and baseball hat. There was Sam in his awful yellow swimsuit.

Loyal friends.

FIND YOUR CHINESE ZODIAC ANIMAL

The Chinese Zodiac uses animal signs in a repeating twelve-year cycle to date years. Find the year you were born to find your Chinese animal horoscope. The Chinese New Year is at the end of January, so if you were born in January, your animal horoscope is the previous year's.

RAT

1984, 1996

People born in the Year of the Rat are charming, thrifty, and love to gossip. They also have an annoying habit of chewing through boxes of snack crackers.

OX

1985, 1997

Year of the Ox people can be thoughtful, steady, and easygoing. They make good friends because they can also pull very heavy boxes very long distances.

TIGER

1986, 1998

Those born in the Year of the Tiger are powerful, sensitive, and sometimes short-tempered. But it's kind of creepy the way they can blend into the living room furniture and then pounce on you.

RABBIT

1987, 1999

If you were born in the Year of the Rabbit, there is a good chance that you are talented, kind, and clever. There is also a good chance that you will have big ears and like carrots.

DRAGON

1988, 2000

Energetic, excitable, and brave are three good words to describe people born in the Year of the Dragon. Scaly, smelly, and scary are three more.

SNAKE

1989, 2001

People born in the Year of the Snake shouldn't mention it too often. They are likely to be deep, wise, and good-looking. But how do you explain all of those big hunks of shed skin in your bedroom?

HORSE

1990, 2002

Those born in the Year of the Horse are popular, cheerful, and very independent. Their only weakness is their habit of eating an awful lot of oatmeal. Oh, and that smell.

RAM

1991, 2003

Elegant and artistic, Year of the Ram people are also often shy and timid. But don't turn your back on them. Because if you do, you will get rammed.

MONKEY

1992, 2004

If you were born in the Year of the Monkey, you are most likely skillful, inventive, and original. But do you always have to jump on the furniture and scratch your armpit? That is not very attractive.

ROOSTER

1993, 2005

Year of the Rooster people are deep thinkers. They can sometimes be difficult to get along with because they always think they are right. And then there is that bad habit of making way too much noise every darn morning, right when the sun comes up.

DOG

1994, 2006

Trustworthy, loyal, and helpful—sounds like something from the Boy Scouts, but is a good description of people born in the Year of the Dog. You should also add: sloppy, stubborn, and likely to drink water from the toilet.

BOAR

1995, 2007

The last animal in the Chinese Zodiac, and a little touchy about it. Those born in the Year of the Boar are honest, strong, kind, and very mad if you call them a Pig. It's Boar. B-O-A-R. Got it?